INFINITE CRISIS
AFTERMATH
THE BATTLE FOR
BLÜDHAVEN

Following the world-shattering events known as the **Infinite Crisis**, the stories of the DC Universe catapulted ahead one year where the **World's Greatest Superheroes** continue their adventures in new settings and situations!

Dan DiDio Senior VP-Executive Editor • **Tom Palmer, Jr.** Editor-original series

Bob Harras Group Editor-collected edition • **Robbin Brosterman** Senior Art Director

Paul Levitz President & Publisher • **Georg Brewer** VP-Design & DC Direct Creative

Richard Bruning Senior VP-Creative Director • **Patrick Caldon** Executive VP-Finance & Operations

Chris Caramalis VP-Finance • **John Cunningham** VP-Marketing

Terri Cunningham VP-Managing Editor • **Stephanie Fierman** Senior VP-Sales & Marketing

Alison Gill VP-Manufacturing • **Hank Kanalz** VP-General Manager, WildStorm

Jim Lee Editorial Director-WildStorm • **Paula Lowitt** Senior VP-Business & Legal Affairs

MaryEllen McLaughlin VP-Advertising & Custom Publishing

Gregory Noveck Senior VP-Creative Affairs • **John Nee** VP-Business Development

Cheryl Rubin Senior VP-Brand Management

Jeff Trojan VP-Business Development, DC Direct • **Bob Wayne** VP-Sales

Cover illustration by **Daniel Acuña**

Publication design by **Amie Brockway-Metcalf**

Logo Design by **John J. Hill**

CRISIS AFTERMATH: THE BATTLE FOR BLÜDHAVEN

Published by DC Comics. Cover, introduction and compilation copyright © 2007 DC Comics. All Rights Reserved.

Originally published in single magazine form in CRISIS AFTERMATH: THE BATTLE FOR BLÜDHAVEN 1-6.

Copyright © 2006 DC Comics. All Rights Reserved.

All characters, their distinctive likenesses and related elements featured in this publication are trademarks of DC Comics. The stories, characters and incidents featured in this publication are entirely fictional.

DC Comics does not read or accept unsolicited submissions of ideas, stories or artwork.

DC Comics, 1700 Broadway, New York, NY 10019

A Warner Bros. Entertainment Company

Printed in Canada. First Printing.

ISBN: 1-4012-1199-2

ISBN 13: 978-1-4012-1199-8

CRISIS AFTERMATH: THE BATTLE FOR BLÜDHAVEN

written by
Justin Gray and Jimmy Palmiotti

layouts by
Dan Jurgens (chapters 1-4 and 6) and Gordon Purcell (chapter 5)

finishes by
Jimmy Palmiotti

Colored by Javi Montes
Lettered by Pat Brosseau and Nick J. Napolitano
Covers by Daniel Acuña

PREVIOUSLY IN THE DC UNIVERSE

Blüdhaven existed for years in the shadow of its more prosperous neighbor, Gotham City, but was eventually able to surpass it when it came to crime, murder and police corruption. But unlike Gotham, Blüdhaven lacked a protector. Then came Nightwing. Dick Grayson, Batman's first Robin, had long ago grown out of the shadow of the Bat and established his own identity as a hero. Following a clue in a murder, Dick found in Blüdhaven a city he could call his own to protect, and one that desperately needed him.

As Nightwing, Dick devoted his nights to taking down Blüdhaven's head of organized crime, the super-powered Blockbuster. By day Dick took a job with the Blüdhaven police department, hoping to root out the rampant corruption from the inside. After long, hard years in which many of those close to Dick became casualties of his struggle with Blockbuster, the crime lord was killed by the vigilante Tarantula. Into the vacuum of power stepped Nightwing's old nemesis Deathstroke, who had allied himself with Lex Luthor's Society of Supervillains.

Nightwing went undercover in Deathstroke's organization and nearly succeeded in turning Deathstroke's daughter, Ravager, against him. The two struck a deal — Nightwing would leave the girl alone if Deathstroke promised not to interfere in Blüdhaven, and to keep all metahuman villains out of the city. At long last, Dick had freed Blüdhaven from the crime and the corruption that had held it in check for so long.

But his victory was tragically short-lived. Deathstroke double-crossed Nightwing, and Luthor's Society committed an unthinkable act — they dropped the toxic giant Chemo onto the city like a giant chemical bomb. In an instant 100,000 were killed, the city was rendered uninhabitable and all of Dick's efforts were for nothing. Superman, Batman, the Teen Titans and others did their part to aid the survivors, but the heroes were soon caught up in the Infinite Crisis — a struggle that threatened to destroy the entire universe.

The aftermath of the Crisis left Superman, Batman and Wonder Woman missing for an entire year, and Blüdhaven found itself in the hands of the U.S. government. Now a secretive government group called S.H.A.D.E. (The Super Human Advanced Defense Executive) has taken control of operations in Blüdhaven, while a group of refugees waits outside the city walls for permission to return to their homes. Tensions are rising, and only the Brooklyn-based golem known as the Monolith is there to provide crowd control. As conflict becomes inevitable, the question on everyone's mind is

WHERE ARE THE SUPERHEROES?

CHAPTER 1

BLUDHAVEN CITY LIMITS

AMID THE CHAOS AND CARNAGE, SURVIVORS TRIED AS BEST THEY COULD TO GRASP THE MAGNITUDE OF WHAT HAD HAPPENED.

THE PRESIDENT DECLARED A STATE OF EMERGENCY AND RELIEF BEGAN POURING IN, FIRST FROM THE NATION, AND THEN THE WORLD. DUE TO THE TOXIC NATURE OF THE CHEMO BLAST, A WALL WAS ERECTED AROUND THE CITY WITHIN THE FIRST THIRTY-SIX HOURS.

TRIAGE SITES WERE SET UP ALONG THE WALL. AMERICANS CAME FROM EVERY CORNER OF THE COUNTRY TO HELP AS BEST THEY COULD. THE HEART OF THE NATION WAS CUT SO DEEPLY THAT MANY DOUBTED SHE WOULD EVER HEAL.

WE ARE DYING!

SAVE US

HELP US!

WHY ARE WE STILL LOCKED OUT?

WHY CAN'T WE COLLECT OUR THINGS AND BURY OUR DEAD?

THIS DOESN'T LOOK LIKE AMERICA TO ME. OUR OWN GOVERNMENT PUSHED US OUT AND BUILT A WALL TO MAKE SURE WE DIDN'T GET BACK IN.

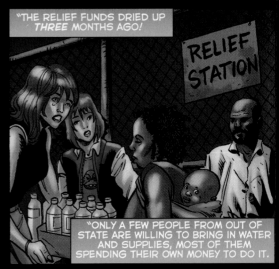

"THE RELIEF FUNDS DRIED UP *THREE* MONTHS AGO!

RELIEF STATION

"ONLY A FEW PEOPLE FROM OUT OF STATE ARE WILLING TO BRING IN WATER AND SUPPLIES, MOST OF THEM SPENDING THEIR OWN MONEY TO DO IT.

"WE'RE KEPT OUT HERE IN THIS INTERNMENT CAMP AND EVERYONE IS GETTING DESPERATE. THEY'RE TURNING AGAINST EACH OTHER FOR SCRAPS OF FOOD.

"INSTEAD OF THE *JUSTICE LEAGUE* OR THE *TEEN TITANS* HELPING TO KEEP THE PEACE, WE HAVE A PAIR OF SOCIAL WORKERS AND A GOLEM FROM NEW YORK."

SOMEONE HAS TO DO SOMETHING. SOMEONE HAS TO STAND UP AND *CHALLENGE* THESE FASCISTS.

I WAS CAUGHT IN THE BLAST FOR A PURPOSE. AT FIRST I DIDN'T UNDERSTAND, BUT NOW I REALIZE THIS POWER WAS GIVEN TO ME TO ILLUMINATE THE TRUTH, TO BE A *FIREBRAND*.

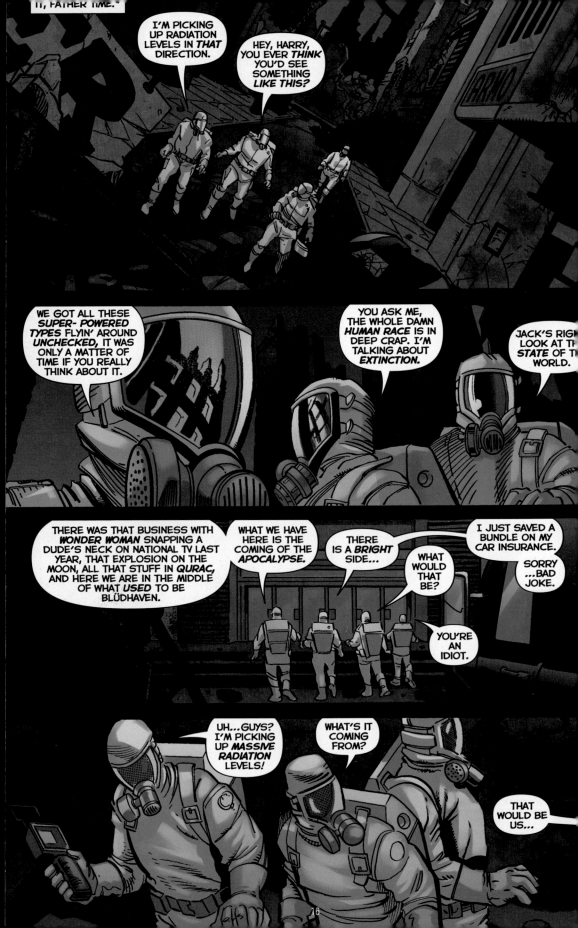

PEOPLE MUST CALM DOWN!

I AM *FIREBRAND* AND THIS IS A *FREE COUNTRY,* NOT A DICTATOR-SHIP!

FIREBRAND IS RIGHT! WE'RE TAKING BACK *BLÜDHAVEN!*

HEY! NO GUNS!

KACHOW

IT'S THE ONLY WAY TO GET THEIR ATTENTION!

UNH!

GET THOSE PEOPLE OUT OF HERE!

HE'S DAMAGED THE CLOAKING UNIT, GARDNER!

KRUNK

BOOM

THAT WASN'T THERE *TWO SECONDS* AGO!

IT DOESN'T LOOK LIKE ANY GOVERNMENT INSTALLATION I'VE SEEN.

MAYBE IT HAS SOMETHING TO DO WITH THAT UNDERGROUND RAIL--

WHO CARES! NUCLEAR LEGION...KILL *EVERYONE!* WE'LL SORT IT OUT LATER!

--ARRRRR!!!

SSSZZZZLL

CHAPTER
2

Where is the protector
of Blüdhaven?

I REALLY *DISLIKE* THOSE PEOPLE.

FORGET ABOUT THEM AND FOCUS...*MAJOR VICTORY* IS ESCAPING! NOW THE FEDS WILL KNOW WE'RE HERE AND SEND MORE AMERICAN LATEX AFTER US.

JUST A SECOND. I WANT A LOOK AT ONE OF THESE SUITS OF ARMOR. THE SOCIETY MIGHT WANT THEM.

WAIT. WHAT'S THAT *NOISE?*

CHA-

THOOM

PING
PING

SONOVA...!

THAT'S IT!

MY BLOOD ALCOHOL LEVELS ARE *DANGEROUSLY* LOW, THERE ISN'T A DRUG DEALER IN FIFTY MILES OF THIS PLACE AND I'M *SERIOUSLY* CONSIDERING *BAILING* ON YOU IDIOTS.

LET'S GET WHAT WE'RE HERE FOR AND GO.

WE'VE **SUPPRESSED** THE UPRISING, FATHER TIME.

I WISH WE COULD THROW A LITTLE MUSTARD GAS DOWN THERE AND BE DONE WITH IT.

SIR?

LOOK AT THEM ...**MAGGOTS** SQUIRMING IN THE MUD.

WE NEED THE BOOT OF A WAR GOD TO STAMP DOWN UPON THE WEAK SYCOPHANTS THAT ARE EATING AWAY AT THIS COUNTRY.

"I WANT A COMPLETE MEDIA **BLACKOUT.** IF YOU SEE ANYONE IN A COSTUME, YOU SHOOT TO KILL. I DON'T GIVE A DAMN IF IT'S GREEN LANTERN, SUPERMAN OR THE WHOLE JUSTICE LEAGUE RIDING MAGIC PONIES."

MOVE BACK! CLEAR THIS AREA!

BACK OFF, WE'RE HELPING PATCH UP THE PEOPLE YOU MORONS SHOT!

THAT'S IT, YOU'RE UNDER **ARREST!**

GET OFFA ME, JERK!

LET GO OF MY FRIEND TILT.

NO MORE TROUBLE. **HELP** PEOPLE.

JESUS...

MY **BOYFRIEND'S** HERE AND HE'S GOING TO KICK YOUR **BUTT.**

MOVE EVERYONE BACK **BEHIND** THE PERIMETER AS SOON AS POSSIBLE.

HEY, THEY'VE HAD **A YEAR** TO CLEAN UP BLÜDHAVEN AND STILL NONE OF US ARE **ALLOWED** BACK IN.

I GREW UP IN THIS TOWN. NOW THE GOVERNMENT, THE PEOPLE WE PAY WITH OUR TAXES ARE KEEPING US OUT? **MEANWHILE,** WHERE ARE THE SO-CALLED HEROES? WHERE IS **NIGHTWING?** WHERE'S THE JUSTICE LEAGUE OF AMERICA?

IT SEEMS TO ME THEY SHOULD BE HERE BECAUSE THERE'S A HUGE **INJUSTICE...** RIGHT HERE AT THE WALL. I'M TELLING YOU WE NEED TO DO SOMETHING!

LIVE

WGBS

TELL ME AGAIN HOW WE DID THE *RIGHT THING* BY LEAVING BLÜDHAVEN.

THE GOVERNMENT ASKED US TO LEAVE. WE HAVE TO TRUST THAT THEY KNOW WHAT THEY'RE DOING, ROBIN.

THAT FIREBRAND GUY HAS A POINT. WE SHOULD BE DOING *SOMETHING.*

LIKE WHAT, RAVAGER? OUR GOVERNMENT HAS BLÜDHAVEN ON LOCKDOWN. YOU HEARD THE PRESIDENT THE OTHER NIGHT. NO ONE IS ALLOWED IN OR OUT.

I THINK IT'S OBVIOUS THEY DON'T HAVE A CLUE, WONDER GIRL.

I DON'T LIKE SITTING HERE DOING *NOTHING* WHEN SOLDIERS ARE SHOOTING *INNOCENT PEOPLE* IN THE STREETS. SOMEHOW THAT DOESN'T FEEL LIKE GOOD NATIONAL SECURITY.

WHAT'S THE *POINT* OF BEING *TITANS* IF WE'RE NOT GOING TO STAND UP FOR WHAT'S RIGHT? *SUPERMAN* LEFT US IN *CHARGE...*

ROBIN, WE WERE *ASKED* TO LEAVE BY A *HIGHER* AUTHORITY. NOT EVEN *SUPERMAN* CAN CHANGE GOVERNMENT POLICY.

HOW CAN YOU BE SO *LEVEL* HEADED?

I DON'T SEE THEM THROWING *FIREBRAND* AND *MONOLITH* IN JAIL. THERE'S NO HARM IN GOING TO THE WALL AND ASKING QUESTIONS.

I WANT TO TALK TO *FIREBRAND* FIRST. IT COULD BE HE'S STARTING *TROUBLE* WHERE THERE ISN'T ANY.

KID DEVIL'S RIGHT. I SAY WE GO.

ALL DEAD AND YOU RAN AWAY?

YES SIR. I MEAN NO, SIR. THEY WERE KILLED BY THE *NUCLEAR LEGION.*

ALSO, THE UNDERGROUND RAILROAD WAS ACCIDENTALLY *EXPOSED* DURING OUR BATTLE.

THEY CALLED THEMSELVES THE *ATOMIC KNIGHTS* AND ARE LED BY SOMEONE NAMED *GARDNER GRAYLE.* THEY HAVE HIGHLY ADVANCED *ARMORED SUITS* AND CLOAKING TECHNOLOGY...THAT'S WHY WE CAN'T FIND THEM.

PRETENDING TO BE REFUGEES...SNEAKY BASTARDS.

I'LL NEED *REINFORCEMENTS* TO TRACK THEM DOWN.

YOU'LL HAVE THEM. THANKS TO THE RIOT AT THE WALL, YOU'VE BEEN ABSORBED INTO THE *SUPER HUMAN ADVANCED DEFENSE EXECUTIVE.*

THE *WHAT?*

EXACTLY. MEET ME IN THE BRIEFING ROOM AT OH EIGHT HUNDRED.

HOW CAN YOU BE SO DAMN *CALM* ABOUT THIS, *GARDNER?*

MARENE, YOU UNDERSTAND *WHY* WE'VE BEEN ACTIVATED.

ALL I *NDERSTAND* PEOPLE ARE *DYING* AND *HAT'S* LEFT OF THIS CITY IS A WAR ZONE.

IF WE DON'T ACT, THE REST OF THE WORLD WILL SUFFER THE *SAME* FATE AS BLÜDHAVEN.

I'M PICKING UP SEVEN HEAT SIGNATURES AHEAD.

SO YOU HAVE VISIONS OF THE FUTURE AND WE ARE ALL PART OF SOMETHING LARGER ... IN THE MEANTIME, TRY NOT TO FORGET ABOUT THE SMALLER THINGS.

THE SMALL *HINGS* ARE WHAT I'M *TRYING* TO PROTECT.

STAY AWAY! WE WON'T LET THE *BLACK BARON* TAKE OUR CHILDREN!

I DON'T KNOW WHO YOU'RE TALKING ABOUT.

WE'VE COME TO GET YOU SAFELY OUT OF THE CITY.

THE UNDERGROUND RAILROAD EVERYONE TALKS ABOUT?

YES. WHO IS THIS *BLACK BARON*?

HE'S GOT ALL OF THE *MEDICINE* AND *DRY GOODS*.

AND IF YOU DON'T WORK FOR HIM, WELL... YOU STARVE. HE ALSO TAKES THE *CHILDREN*... IN CASE THE BOMB CHANGED THEM. SIR...WE'VE SEEN SOME VERY *STRANGE* THINGS IN THE LAST SIX MONTHS.

HOW *MANY* PEOPLE DOES BLACK BARON HAVE WORKING FOR HIM?

I DON'T KNOW, A HUNDRED...MAYBE MORE. THEY'RE EVERYWHERE IF YOU LOOK CLOSE ENOUGH.

HE SET UP A COMPOUND A COUPLE O BLOCKS OVE AT *RABE* HOSPITAL.

HE AND HIS MEN...THEY GOT A LOT OF WEAPONS.

ROUNDTABLE, THIS IS GRAYLE.

THIS IS ROUNDTABLE. GO AHEAD.

I NEED AN EVAC SENT TO MY LOCATION. I ALSO WANT A DETACHMENT SENT TO *INVESTIGATE* RABE HOSPITAL. YOUR TARGET IS CALLED BLACK BARON. EXPECT *RESISTANCE*.

WE HAVE LOCATED THE MILITARY EXPERIMENTAL INSTALLATION WHERE THE *RADIOACTIVE ANOMALY* IS CENTERED. ROUNDTABLE REQUESTS YOU INVESTIGATE.

DOWNLOAD THE *COORDINATES* TO MY SUIT.

IS THIS THEM?

WHUP WHUP WHUP

I SAID NO TALKING.

SO THIS YEAR'S LOOK IS COLONEL SANDERS, TIME? THERE BETTER BE A *DAMNED* CUP OF *COFFEE* WAITING FOR ME.

I'VE GOT A *HANGOVER*, I'M CRANKY, AND I TOLD YOU I'M *NEVER* OUT OF BED *BEFORE* NOON.

YOU'RE NOT GOING TO RECEIVE ANY *SPECIAL TREATMENT* JUST BECAUSE YOUR FATHER'S A *SENATOR*, MISS KNIGHT.

SINCE WHEN IS COFFEE SPECIAL TREATMENT, YOU GRISTLY OLD BASTARD?

WHERE IS THE SECRET WEAPON?

STILL SLEEPING AFTER A SEVENTY-TWO-HOUR ASSASSINATION RUN IN BERLIN.

AMERIKA

SO THIS GUY WAS CREATED IN THE *NINETEEN THIRTIES* BY YOUR GRANDMOTHER USING SOME KIND OF *JEWISH MAGIC*?

THAT'S PRETTY TRIPPY.

MY NAME IS PETER OR *MONOLITH*. I CAN TALK AND LISTEN VERY GOOD.

SORRY, PETER.

PETE REGAINED HIS MEMORIES ON CHRISTMAS MORNING. HOW'S THAT FOR A PRESENT. SO WHAT'S YOUR DEAL? A LOT OF PEOPLE WERE HURT WHEN YOU STARTED JUMPING AROUND LIKE A BALLET DANCER ON FIRE.

MY DEAL IS THAT I SEEM TO BE THE *ONLY GUY* ASKING QUESTIONS. LET ME ASK YOU SOMETHING, TILT. DON'T YOU THINK IT'S *STRANGE* THAT THE CITY IS STILL CLOSED OFF?

NOT WHEN YOU CONSIDER THE *RADIATION POISONING* WE KEEP HEARING ABOUT.

HOW DO WE *KNOW* THAT'S REAL?

IF YOU LOOK AT *CHERNOBYL*, THERE'S A LOT OF RADIATION THAT LEAKED OUT AND WAS DANGEROUS TO PEOPLE FOR *HUNDREDS OF MILES*, BUT HERE WE ARE JUST OUTSIDE THE CITY BEING EXPOSED TO WHO KNOWS WHAT.

CONSPIRACY THEORIES ASIDE, FIREBRAND, WE'RE JUST *VOLUNTEERS.* WE CAME FROM NEW YORK TO HELP PEOPLE IN NEED. WE HAVE NO *IDEA* WHAT HAPPENED INSIDE THE CITY OR WHAT TO *DO* ABOUT IT.

I'VE MET A FEW GUYS LIKE YOU WITH THE *CRAZY POWERS* AND GOOFY HALLOWEEN COSTUMES.

THE ONE THING I'VE LEARNED ABOUT YOU PEOPLE IS THE TROUBLE ALWAYS GETS *WORSE* WHEN YOU'RE INVOLVED.

HEY, THIS *DISASTER* IS WHAT GAVE ME MY POWER. I'M JUST AS MUCH A *VICTIM* AS ANYONE ELSE AND I'M SICK OF IT. I WANT TO BE PROACTIVE.

IF THAT MEANS DISGUISING MY IDENTITY AND *USING* THOSE POWERS TO GET ANSWERS, THEN I'M GOING TO DO IT. LOOK AT MONOLITH. IS HE ANY DIFFERENT?

WELL... FOR *ONE THING,* HE DIDN'T START A RIOT THAT RESULTED IN PEOPLE GETTING *SHOT.*

FREEDOM'S RING NO LONGER EXISTS. YOU ARE ALL MEMBERS OF *S.H.A.D.E.* NOW. I WANT TO INTRODUCE YOU TO YOUR *NEWLY RESURRECTED* FIELD LEADER...

MAJOR FORCE.

LET'S BEGIN.

THE BLUE AREAS ARE *UNSECURED,* FILLED WITH POTENTIAL META-HUMANS AND CIVILIAN SQUATTERS WHO *REFUSE* TO LEAVE. WE OCCUPY THE RED, AND THE YELLOW ARE VACANT AS FAR AS WE KNOW.

ACCORDING TO *MAJOR VICTORY,* THERE ARE AN UNKNOWN NUMBER OF TECHNOLOGICALLY ADVANCED INSURGENTS CALLED THE *ATOMIC KNIGHTS* OPERATING IN THE BLUE AREAS.

I WANT YOU TO STAMP OUT THESE COCKROACHES AND SECURE THE CITY.

CAN WE KILL THE *UNCOOPERATIVE?*

SLOWLY AND WITH GREAT VIGOR, *MAJOR FORCE,* JUST BRING BACK A FEW *HOSTAGES* FOR INTERROGATION.

GO RIGHT IN, SIR.

WHAT IS THIS PLACE?

THANK YOU, SOLDIER.

WE'RE NOT THE ONLY ONES *COLLECTING* METAS FROM THE CITY.

THEY SEEM TO BE *EXPERIMENTING* ON THEM.

PUTZ.

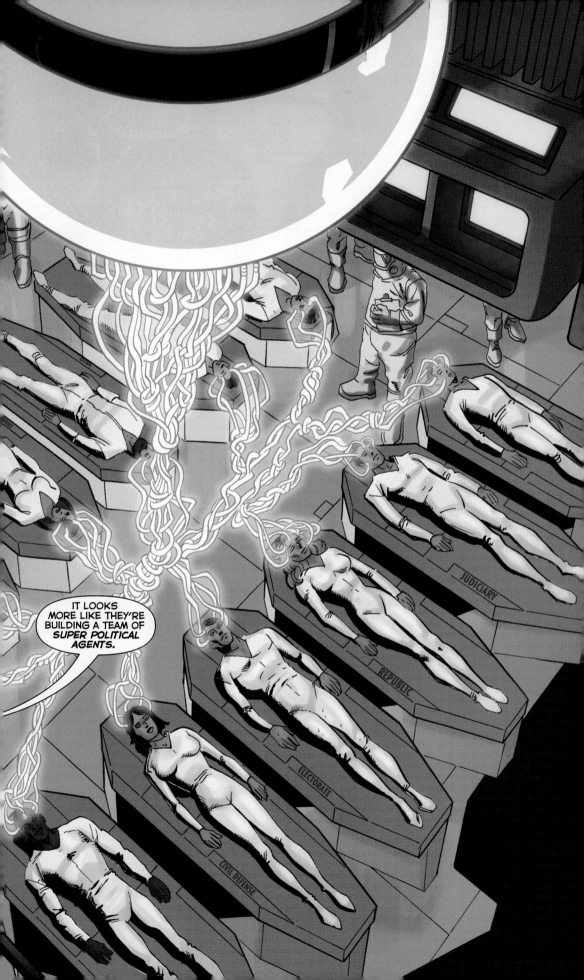

ADMINISTER THE RADIATION TREATMENT.

AT EASE.

ENERGY LEVELS ARE OFF THE CHARTS! THE ARMOR IS BARELY ABLE TO WITHSTAND THE RADIATION LEVELS!

STAY CALM, THE *ARMOR* WILL HOLD.

SIR...

WHAT IS IT, SOLDIER?

PLEASE HOLD, ARMOR!

RECORD AND TRANSMIT TO ROUNDTABLE!

CHAPTER 3

INTRUDER ALERT LAB SIX. LOCKDOWN INITIATED.

DAMN! WE'LL HAVE TO COME BACK FOR HIM!

THE HATCH IS SHUT! WE NEED ANOTHER WAY OUT!

NO SWEAT--

I'LL MAKE ONE.

KSSSSS

INTRUDER ALERT LAB SIX. LOCKDOWN INITIATED.

WHAT THE HELL ARE THEY DOING IN THIS PLACE?

NO TIME FOR THIS NOW...KEEP MOVING!

CURIOUS ARMOR. NON-TERRESTRIAL IN ORIGIN. INITIATING RECORDING FOR FATHER TIME.

53

ARE YOU *CRAZY?* THEY'LL START SHOOTING AGAIN!

SOMEONE HAS TO STAND UP TO THEM!

GET BACK!

THIS IS AN ACT OF TREASON!

THE PEOPLE HAVE A *RIGHT* TO KNOW WHAT'S HAPPENING BEYOND THIS WALL!

YOU CAN'T WRAP YOUR-SELVES IN THE FLAG AND ACCUSE EVERYONE ELSE OF TREASON JUST BECAUSE YOU HAVE A *GUN!*

CAN'T YOU SEE WHAT'S HAPPENING? NEW LEVELS OF SECRET GOVERNMENT ARE EMERGING FROM EACH NEW DISAS--

DO YOU HAVE ANY *IDEA* HOW *CRAZY* YOU SOUND?

AMERIKA

FWUMP

DON'T YOU REALIZE YOU'RE PUTTING PEOPLE IN DANGER WITH THIS *INSANE* BEHAVIOR?

WHAT'S *INSANE* IS THAT SELF-PROCLAIMED HEROES *LIKE YOU* AREN'T GETTING INVOLVED IN WHAT MAY BE THE BIGGEST *CRIME* IN AMERICAN HISTORY! WHERE HAVE YOU BEEN FOR THE PAST YEAR?

CIVIL LIBERTIES ARE BEING *DESTROYED*, MARTIAL LAW HAS BEEN *ENACTED* AND WHAT DO YOU DO ABOUT ALL THE *LIES* WE'VE ALL HAD TO SWALLOW?

YOU DO *NOTHING*!

YOU NEED TO *CALM DOWN*.

WE'RE NOT *AUTHORIZED* MEMBERS OF ANY POLICE FORCE. IN CASE YOU DIDN'T NOTICE, THAT MEANS WE *CAN'T* GO AGAINST THE *GOVERNMENT* SIMPLY BECAUSE WE DISAGREE WITH THEIR POLICY.

DON'T GIVE ME THAT BULL, ROBIN! THAT'S *EXACTLY* WHAT WE *SHOULD* BE DOING!

I CAN'T BELIEVE THIS... YOU, BATMAN AND THE RES HAVE BEEN CONTRADICTING LAW ENFORCEMENT SINCE THE DAY YOU *DECIDED* TO WEAR A MASK!

YOUR ENTIRE *PHILOSOPHY* IS FOUNDED ON THE IDEA THAT LAW ENFORCEMENT AND MILITARY ARE NOT ONLY *INCAPABLE* OF PROTECTING PEOPLE BUT ALSO *CORRUPT* TO THE POINT WHERE *VIGILANTES* HAVE TO TAKE MATTERS INTO THEIR OWN HANDS!

THIS IS NO DIFFERENT.

I UNDERSTAND WHAT YOU'RE SAYING, BUT THE REALITY IS THAT THINGS ARE MUCH MORE *COMPLICATED* THAN THAT.

THERE ARE LAWS AND RULES AND A *CONSTITUTION* TO UPHOLD.

TELL ME, *CYBORG*, WHERE DOES SAY IN THE CONSTITUTION THAT T GOVERNMENT CAN LOCK DOWN A *ENTIRE CITY*, FORCE PEOPLE FRO THEIR *HOMES* AND SHOOT THEM IN THE STREET?

FIREBRAND IS *RIGHT*. TH AIN'T JUST MATTER OF CIVIL RIGHTS

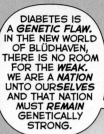
DIABETES IS A *GENETIC FLAW*. IN THE NEW WORLD OF BLÜDHAVEN, THERE IS NO ROOM FOR THE *WEAK*. WE ARE A *NATION* UNTO OURSELVES AND THAT NATION MUST *REMAIN* GENETICALLY STRONG.

PLEASE! SHE'LL *DIE* WITHOUT YOUR HELP!

I WILL NOT HELP HER TO LIVE. IF YOU'RE *STRONG*, YOU CAN JOIN MY ARMY TO HELP *DEFEND* OUR NATION FROM THE *OUTSIDERS*.

JOIN YOUR ARMY? YOU'RE INSANE!

THIS ISN'T A *NATION*! IT'S A BOMBED-OUT CITY WHERE PEOPLE ARE *DYING* FROM *RADIATION POISONING*!

YOU *TWISTED BASTARD*! IF YOU DON'T GIVE ME WHAT I NEED--

ENOUGH.

AAAAARRGGH!

FWAAASH

I LOVE YOU GIRLS, BUT THE SPOKEN WORD BIOGRAPHY EVERY TIME SOMEONE WALKS INTO THIS ROOM IS GETTING A LITTLE...*EMBARRASSING*.

SORRY, BARON. WE ONLY WANT TO SING YOUR PRAISES.

EVERYONE SHOULD KNOW YOU'RE THE LEADER OF THE NEW REVOLUTION.

IT'S ALL RIGHT, GIRLS. ONCE THE *BLÜDNATION* IS COMPLETE AND ALL THE *CHILDREN* OF THE BOMB ARE *UNITED*...

THE *WHOLE* WORLD WILL KNOW MY NAME.

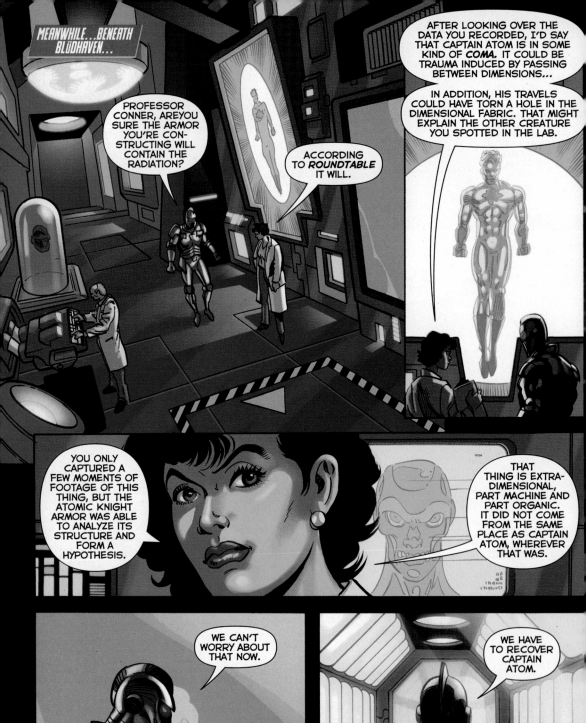

PROFESSOR CONNER, ARE YOU SURE THE ARMOR YOU'RE CONSTRUCTING WILL CONTAIN THE RADIATION?

ACCORDING TO *ROUNDTABLE* IT WILL.

AFTER LOOKING OVER THE DATA YOU RECORDED, I'D SAY THAT CAPTAIN ATOM IS IN SOME KIND OF *COMA*. IT COULD BE TRAUMA INDUCED BY PASSING BETWEEN DIMENSIONS...

IN ADDITION, HIS TRAVELS COULD HAVE TORN A HOLE IN THE DIMENSIONAL FABRIC. THAT MIGHT EXPLAIN THE OTHER CREATURE YOU SPOTTED IN THE LAB.

YOU ONLY CAPTURED A FEW MOMENTS OF FOOTAGE OF THIS THING, BUT THE ATOMIC KNIGHT ARMOR WAS ABLE TO ANALYZE ITS STRUCTURE AND FORM A HYPOTHESIS.

THAT THING IS EXTRA-DIMENSIONAL, PART MACHINE AND PART ORGANIC. IT DID NOT COME FROM THE SAME PLACE AS CAPTAIN ATOM, WHEREVER THAT WAS.

WE CAN'T WORRY ABOUT THAT NOW.

WE HAVE TO RECOVER CAPTAIN ATOM.

IT'S QUIET... I DON'T SEE ANY SOLDIERS.

I'M NOT PICKING UP ANY RADIATION EITHER.

747

THAT'S BECAUSE THERE *ISN'T* ANY.

WE DON'T KNOW THAT FOR SURE.

HOLD IT!

IT'S ALL RIGHT. WE'RE NOT GOING TO HURT YOU.

WE KNOW WHAT YOU PEOPLE DO. YOU BETTER LEAVE--

WHAT ARE YOU TALKING ABOUT?

YOU'RE WITH FREEDOM'S RING, AREN'T YOU?

WE'RE THE TEEN TITANS.

RIGHT...WE KNOW YOU'RE GOVERNMENT METAS SENT TO ROUND US UP. WE'RE NOT GONNA BE LAB RATS. WE'LL *DIE* FIRST.

I DON'T KNOW WHAT YOU'RE TALKING ABOUT.

NOW DO YOU BELIEVE ME, ROBIN?

NONE OF US HAVE ANY POWERS. NO ONE HAS MUTATED EITHER, SO JUST LEAVE US ALONE. WE'RE ONLY TRYING TO *SURVIVE* OUT HERE.

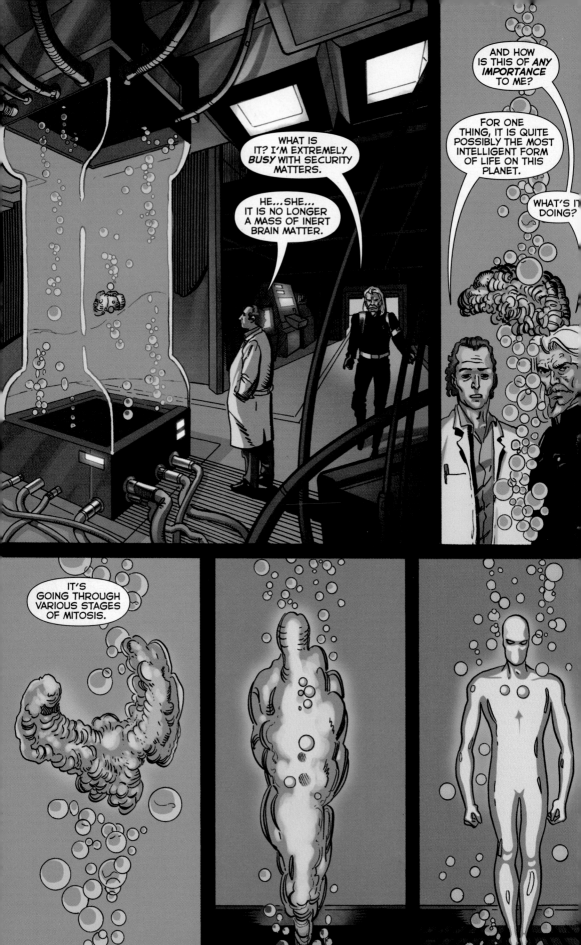

ON MY MARK, BIGFOOT...!

NOW!

LOOKIT ME, AHM THE HERO!

KRRSH

SOMETHING IS BONDING TO THE ARMOR AND INFECTING THE CIRCUITS! SELF-DESTRUCT MODE HAS BEEN OVERRIDDEN!

I NEED HELP!

I GOT THE PRISONER, Y'ALL!

WE NEED SOME BACKUP!

PUT HER DOWN, NOW!

DON'T WORRY, DOLL MAN. I CAN HANDLE THIS.

WHAT THE HELL ARE YOU DOING?

WATCH.

OKAY, HAT WAS JUST NUTS...

WHAT THE *HELL* DID YOU JUST DO, SOLDIER?

HE RIPPED OFF A PIECE OF FINGERNAIL AND KILLED THEM WITH IT!

OKAY, TAY THE HELL VAY FROM ME, EXPLODO.

DON'T BE LIKE THAT.

I'M NOT A DANGER TO YOU...TO *ANY* OF YOU.

YOU'RE A WALKING NUCLEAR BOMB!

YEAH, THAT'S KIND F WHY THEY CALL ME THE HUMAN BOMB.

WHATEVER. THANKS TO DOLL MAN, WE'VE COMPLETED OUR MISSION AND CAPTURED AN ATOMIC KNIGHT.

LET'S BRING HER BACK TO FATHER TIME FOR INTERROGATION.

YOU GUYS AREN'T BEING FAIR. I CAN'T HELP WHAT I'VE BECOME.

YOU'RE...

A...

FREAK...

WHAT HAPPENS IF HE...YA KNOW...HAS GAS, Y'ALL? WE GONNA DIE OF NUCLEAR FALLOUT?

HOW THE HELL DID I END UP ON THIS TEAM!?

CHAPTER 4

SONIC SWEEP INITIATED.

ARRRGGH!

WAYNE AND HOLLIS, OPEN A DOOR!

WE NEED TO GET INSIDE!

ONE DOOR COMING UP.

CHOOM

SCANNERS INDICATE WE'VE GOT MORE *TROUBLE* HEADING OUR WAY OUTSIDE. LOOKS LIKE A BLACKHAWK GUNSHIP.

DOUGLAS--

I'M ON IT, GARDNER... *NOBODY* PANIC.

ENGAGING LOCALIZED E.M.P.

GOOD JOB.

ROUNDTABLE, THIS IS GRAYLE. WE HAVE ACQUIRED CAPTAIN ATOM AND ARE PROCEEDING TO THE CASTLE.

CONFIRMED.

THE *TEEN TITANS* HAVE ILLEGALLY INFILTRATED BLÜDHAVEN."

THERE ARE A LOT MORE PEOPLE IN THIS CITY THAN THE NEWS REPORTED.

ISN'T IT *OBVIOUS?* THE CORRUPT GOVERNMENT OFFICIALS ARE ALL IN BED WITH THE MASSIVE CORPORATIONS WHO OWN THE NETWORKS AND THE NEWS MEDIA.

RABE MEMORIAL HOSPITAL

I'M GETTING *TIRED* OF YOUR PARANOID CONSPIRACY THEORIES, FIREBRAND.

WHATEVER THE CASE, BLÜDHAVEN'S DEGENERATED INTO A *WAR ZONE.*

YOU *THINK* THEY'RE GOING TO BE ANY *FRIENDLIER* THAN THE PEOPLE AT THE AIRPORT?

THIS IS A BAD PLACE.

I WOULDN'T COUNT ON IT, CASSIE.

WE'VE GOT COMPANY! GET INSIDE AND TELL THE *BLACK BARON!*

WAIT! DON'T SHOOT! WE'RE NOT HERE TO *HURT* YOU!

GET BACK!

WHAT'S WRONG WITH THOSE PEOPLE?

THEY'RE DESPERATE.

ANNEXED? IS THIS GUY FOR REAL?

OKAAAYY... I HAVE TO SAY IT...THOSE GIRLS ARE THE BOMB!

BLÜDHAVEN HAS BEEN *ANNEXED* IN THE NAME OF THE HOLY BLACK BARON! YOU ARE *VIOLATING* SOVEREIGN LAND GIVEN TO US BY THE BOMB!

YOU HAVE *FIVE SECONDS* TO TURN BACK, OR THE HOLY WAR WILL COMMENCE!

THIS IS GOING TO GET UGLY A HURRY.

TIME'S UP, LADIES. YOU KNOW WHAT TO DO. GODSPEED AND ALL THAT.

FOR THE GOOD OF BLÜDHAVEN.

FOR THE LOVE OF C LORD BLA BARON.

ROBIN, THOSE GIRLS HAVE *EXPLOSIVES* TIED TO THEM.

WANT ME TO *DETONATE* THEM?

STOP IT, RAVAGER...

THIS IS *INSANE.* WHAT ARE WE GOING TO DO?

MONOLITH!

STAY BACK!

STOP THIS!

VIVA LA REVOLUTION!

WE DIE FOR OUR FREEDOM FROM THE OPPRESSORS!

MAY *I* HAVE MERCY ON YOUR SOULS.

CLICK

82

CHOOM

DID HE JUST--?

I'M GONNA HURL...

MONOLITH... H-HE'S SHATTERED...

HOLY WAR HAS BEEN *DECLARED* AND WE ARE UNDER ATTACK! FIGHT THEM! KILL THEM ALL IN MY NAME!

IT LOOKS LIKE *SOMEONE'S* BEEN HANDING OUT THE JESUS JUICE.

TITANS, GET THIS SITUATION UNDER CONTROL!

I'LL HANDLE THE MAIN NUTCASE.

THAT SMELLS DISGUSTING, KID DEVIL.

HRUUHHH?

WHAT DID YOU DO? WE DON'T *KILL* PEOPLE!

WE DIDN'T.

LOOK, AS LONG AS WE'RE AROUND, YOU'RE NOT GOING TO KILL ANYONE, EVEN IF THEY *DESERVE* IT.

THE CIVILIANS ARE OUT OF HARM'S WAY...WHERE'S THE BARON?

I THINK HE LANDED IN HOBOKEN.

THIS WHOLE SITUATION IS A MESS...

I DON'T CARE IF IT'S THE MILITARY, F.B.I. OR C.I.A... WHOEVER IS *IN CHARGE* NEEDS TO ANSWER FOR WHAT'S HAPPENED TO BLÜDHAVEN.

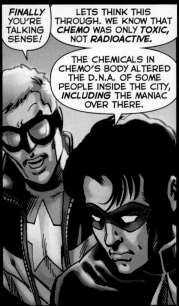

FINALLY YOU'RE TALKING SENSE!

LETS THINK THIS THROUGH. WE KNOW THAT *CHEMO* WAS ONLY *TOXIC,* NOT *RADIOACTIVE.*

THE CHEMICALS IN CHEMO'S BODY ALTERED THE D.N.A. OF SOME PEOPLE INSIDE THE CITY, *INCLUDING* THE MANIAC OVER THERE.

BUT THERE'S *DEFINITELY* RADIATION IN THE CITY.

THE *REALITY* IS THE GOVERNMENT IS DOING SOMETHING MASSIVELY ILLEGAL.

WE DON'T KNOW THAT FOR SURE.

IT'S TIME TO FIND OUT.

I'VE SEEN HIS TECHNOLOGY BEFORE.

AS YOU CAN IMAGINE, I'M *EXTREMELY CURIOUS* ABOUT HOW YOU AND YOUR FRIENDS *ACQUIRED* IT.

GO TO HELL.

LET'S GO TOGETHER.

THIS IS *THE FACE.*

OF COURSE, BY THAT TIME, HE'D ALREADY WORKED HIS WAY THROUGH *FIVE THOUSAND* DETAINEES...BUT, BEING THE ENTERPRISING SORT, FACE TOOK IT UPON HIMSELF TO *BREED* THE PRISONERS LIKE *CATTLE.*

YOU SEE, HE TAKES HIS WORK *VERY SERIOUSLY* AND WITH NO NEW CAPTIVES COMING IN, IT WAS THE ONLY *LOGICAL* THING TO DO.

THERE'S AN AIRPLANE HANGAR *FILLED* WITH MEDICAL JOURNALS DETAILING HIS *ACQUIRED KNOWLEDGE* OF PAIN AND SUFFERING.

WE TRIED TO HAVE THEM TRANSCRIBED INTO *COMPUTER FILES,* BUT EVERYONE WHO READS THEM EVENTUALLY GOES *INSANE.*

WE MET IN A SECRET *UNDERGROUND CONCENTRATION* CAMP IN NINETEEN FIFTY.

SEEMS NO ONE TOLD THE POOR FELLOW WORLD WAR TWO ENDED FIVE YEARS EARLIER.

I'LL LET YOU TWO GET *ACQUAINTED.*

REPLICANT, WHAT WAS THAT?

HUMAN BOMB HAS JUST DESTROYED PHILLIPS STREET.

I'M GLAD HE'S ON THE OTHER SIDE OF TOWN.

REPLICANT, ARE WE GETTING ANY CLOSER TO CAPTAIN ATOM'S LOCATION?

I'M NOT PICKING UP ANY ACTIVITY FROM HIS BRAIN, BUT THE RADIATION SIGNATURE IS STILL HOT.

AT LEAST HE'S STILL IN BLÜDHAVEN.

THE KNIGHTS WILL KEEP HIM HERE. I DON'T BELIEVE THEY WOULD RISK EXPOSING ANY MORE PEOPLE TO RADIATION BEYOND THE WALL.

REPLICANT, WHY IS CAPTAIN ATOM SO IMPORTANT TO FATHER TIME?

THAT'S CLASSIFIED, PHANTOM LADY.

OF COURS

MAJOR FORCE, BE ADVISED THAT THE TEEN TITANS ARE CURRENTLY INSIDE THE CITY. I'M SPREAD TOO THIN SEARCHING FOR ATOMIC KNIGHTS TO PINPOINT THEIR CURRENT LOCATION.

PLEASE TELL ME WE CAN KILL THOSE BRATS.

AVOID ALL CONTACT. CAPTAIN ATOM IS MISSION CRITICAL. WE CANNOT AFFORD EXTERNAL INTERFERENCE THAT WILL DRAW THE ATTENTION OF KNOWN METAS.

REPLICANT, WHAT ARE OUR ORDERS IN THE EVENT OF ACCIDENTAL CONTACT?

THE TEEN TITANS ARE TO BE CAPTURED OR KILLED TO PRESERVE THE INTEGRITY OF THE MISSION.

I VOTE KILL.

WHO ARE THOSE GUYS?

THAT'S A GOOD QUESTION, CONSIDERING THAT MOST OF THEM ARE SUPPOSED TO BE DEAD.

THE ONE THING WE DO KNOW IS THEY'RE WORKING FOR THE GOVERNMENT.

SETTLE DOWN, FIREBRAND. LET ME GO TALK TO THEM.

LOOK OUT!

FZARKK

NO, YOU'RE NOT...

THE SOCIETY *KILLED* PHANTOM LADY.

OKAY. THEN I'M THE NEW AND *IMPROVED* PHANTOM LADY AND YOU'RE NOW TRAPPED BETWEEN THE SECOND AND THIRD DIMENSION.

IN JUST A MINUTE YOU'LL PASS OUT FROM LACK OF OXYGEN.

ROBIN'S DOWN.

IS IT HAPPY HOUR YET?

CYBORG'S DOWN. HOW MANY ARE LEFT?

CHAPTER 5

HURRY UP AND GET THE RESTRAINTS ON THEM. FATHER TIME WANTS THE TITANS RELOCATED TO THE HOLDING AREA IMMEDIATELY.

IF ANY OF YOU FAINT AT THE SIGHT OF YOUR OWN BLOOD, I SUGGEST YOU RUN AWAY AND HIDE!

THUMP

IT'S RAVAGER!

WHERE'D SHE COME FROM?

I'M ACCEPTING APPLICATIONS FOR HOSTAGES AND INFORMANTS, SO THOSE OF YOU WHO ARE INCLINED TO COOPERATE, DROP YOUR WEAPONS AND LIE DOWN ON THE GROUND.

THE REST OF YOU ARE HAMBURGER MEAT.

SOME HERO I'M TURNING OUT TO BE.

YA JUST NEED PRACTICE, ANDRE.

WHO'S THERE?

HOW DO YOU KNOW MY NAME?

WHO? COME OUT WHERE I CAN SEE YOU!

AH NEED YA TA LEAVE BLÜDHAVEN. THERE'S NOT MUCH MORE YA CAN DO FER NOW.

O-KAY, AND WHERE AM I SUPPOSED TO GO, MISTER DISEMBODIED VOICE?

AH KNOW LOTS ABOUT YA, KID. THE REAL QUESTION YA GOTTA BE ASKIN' YERSELF IS WHO WILL CARRY ON THE SPIRIT OF ROD REILLY?

SOUTH. TA THE MIGHTY MISSISSIPPI.

RIGHT...AND THEN I'LL THROW MYSELF IN AND DROWN LIKE JEFF BUCKLEY BECAUSE I'M HEARING VOICES IN MY HEAD. WHO OR WHATEVER YOU ARE...YOU CAN *FORGET* IT.

I'M STAYING HERE AND REPORTING WHAT I'VE SEEN TO THE MEDIA.

LISTEN TA ME, ANDRE. YA BEEN GIVEN POWER AN' A PURPOSE TA DO PRECISELY THAT.

IT AIN'T THE GOVERNMENT YA SHOULD BE FIGHTIN'... ONLY CORRUPT FACTIONS WITHIN IT. THERE ARE MEN WHO WILL COME TO POWER THAT THREATEN LIBERTY.

OF THE PEOPLE
BY THE PEOPLE
AGAINST THE PEOPLE

YOU'RE SURE, ALICE?

POSITIVE. I FELT SOMETHING BAD HAPPEN TO MONOLITH. WE HAVE TO GET IN THERE AND HELP HIM.

BREAKING AND ENTERING. JUST LIKE THE OLD DAYS.

YEAH, ONLY THIS LITTLE ROAD TRIP IS BEHIND ENEMY LINES.

HOW DO WE GET PAST ALL THE G.I. JOES? MAYBE I CAN DISTRACT THEM BY RUNNING TOPLESS IN THE OTHER DIRECTION...

NOT NECESSARY... LOOK, I'M LIKE JAMES GARNER IN "THE GREAT ESCAPE," BABY.

YEAH, BLENDING IN MIGHT BE A BETTER IDEA... I'M EXPECTING COMPLETE MADNESS ON THE OTHER SIDE OF THAT WALL.

GOOD. THIS WAY WE WON'T BE SURPRISED.

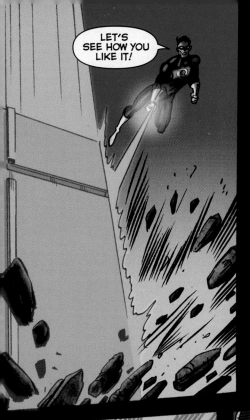

LET'S SEE HOW YOU LIKE IT!

I SPENT MONTHS IN SPACE AS A DECAPITATED HEAD BECAUSE OF THAT WEASEL, RAYNER...

...AND NOW I'M GONNA MURDER EVERY GREEN LANTERN I CAN FIND!

YOU'RE ABOUT TO BE MARKED OFF MY LIST!

CHOOM

COME ON, GET ON YOUR FEET!

THAT'S ENOUGH, FORCE! GET CONTROL OF YOURSELF...THIS IS A BAG AND TAG MISSION.

YOU KNOW, IT JUST OCCURRED TO ME--

WHAT? WHAT ARE YOU GUYS LOOKING AT--?

I'LL TELL YOU WHAT...

YOU'RE A BUTCHERING PSYCHOPATH THAT NEEDS TO BE PUT DOWN!

KLUD

OKAY, IT'S OFFICIAL. YOU GUYS WIN THE CRAZIEST TEAMMATE AWARD. THAT DUDE IS SERIOUSLY ILL.

I THOUGHT IT WUZ KINDA FUNNY.

LESTER, I'M NOT TAKING ORDERS FROM THAT GUY ANYMORE.

ME NEITHER, KID.

I CAN'T BELIEVE YOU'RE SIDING WITH THAT MANIAC, PHANTOM LADY.

I JUST MET THE GUY AND WE DON'T EVEN LIKE EACH OTHER.

MAYBE ITS TIME TO RE-EVALUATE YOUR SITUATION...

CHAPTER 6

ONE YEAR AGO, BLÜDHAVEN WAS NEVER WHAT YOU'D CALL A **SAFE** PLACE TO LIVE.

AFTER DESTRUCTION RAINED DOWN FROM THE SKY IN THE FORM OF **CHEMO**--A CREATURE THAT ALL BUT OBLITERATED THE HEART OF THE CITY--THE DANGER HAS NEVER BEEN GREATER.

THE EXPLOSION CAUSED BY CHEMO RIPPED A HOLE IN THE FABRIC OF SPACE AND TIME, ALLOWING THE DISPLACED HERO **CAPTAIN ATOM** TO RETURN TO HIS HOME WORLD.

HIS WELCOMING PARTY WAS LESS THAN FRIENDLY.

BADLY WOUNDED, HIS BODY CRACKED AND LEAKING RADIATION, CAPTAIN ATOM CAME DANGEROUSLY CLOSE TO REACHING CRITICAL MASS, AN EVENT THAT WOULD HAVE DONE GREATER HARM TO AN ALREADY SHELL-SHOCKED CITY.

SENSORS INDICATE BRAIN ACTIVITY.

WHERE... WHERE AM I?

WELCOME BACK, NATHANIEL CHRISTOPHER ADAM. YOU HAVE RETURNED TO EARTH IN THE TWENTY-FIRST CENTURY. YOU ARE BENEATH WHAT REMAINS OF BLÜDHAVEN.

I...DON'T UNDERSTAND... WHAT HAVE YOU *DONE* TO ME...? AM I A *PRISONER?* WHO THE *HELL* ARE YOU PEOPLE?

THIS...THIS ISN'T *RIGHT.* I CAN'T THINK STRAIGHT...

WARNING. PLEASE CALM DOWN, ADAM. YOUR POWER LEVELS ARE DANGEROUSLY HIGH. THE ARMOR IS RESPONDING TO YOUR HEIGHTENED STRESS LEVELS.

THIS ARMOR IS DIRECTLY INTERFACING WITH MY BRAIN?

THAT IS CORRECT, CAPTAIN ATOM.

SKRAK

TICK TICK

BOOM

TICK TICK

I DON'T EVEN KNOW WHAT I'M DOING HERE.

AND I AIN'T NEVER PLAYED FETCH WITH A WHOLE DOG B'FORE!

LEMME GO, YOU--

REPLICANT, WHAT JUST HAPPENED? WHAT'S OUR STATUS?

THE SITUATION IS DEGRADING RAPIDLY, FATHER TIME. MAJOR FORCE IS UNSTABLE AND TRYING TO KILL EVERYTHING THAT WALKS OR CRAWLS. THE S.H.A.D.E. UNIT HAS JOINED WITH THE TEEN TITANS TO STOP HIM AND THE NUCLEAR LEGION.

DAMMIT! TELL THEM TO BREAK OFF THEIR ATTACK IMMEDIATELY AND RETURN TO BASE FOR EVAC!

WE'RE WITHDRAWING?

THE WELL IS DRY. HAVE ALL UNITS RELOCATE THE METAS WE'VE CREATED TO S.H.A.D.E. HEADQUARTERS.

WAIT, SIR... RADIATION LEVELS INSIDE THE CITY ARE PLUMMETING.

CAPTAIN ATOM IS DEAD?

IF HE CAN BE STOPPED, MAJOR FORCE WILL TAKE THE FALL FOR OUR MAIN OPERATIONS.

NO, I'M PICKING UP LOW-LEVEL BRAIN ACTIVITY. HE'S WOKEN FROM THE COMA.

BRRRRRRRRRRRRRR--SHOOM

ALL OF YOU, LISTEN TO ME. THIS HAS GONE ON LONG ENOUGH. THOSE WHO WANT TO LIVE, LEAVE *NOW!*

BUT NOT YOU, MAJOR FORCE. YOU STAY RIGHT WHERE YOU ARE!

THAT VOICE--? CAPTAIN ATOM?

I DON'T TAKE ORDERS FROM YOU!

YOU HAVE BEEN A BLIGHT ON THE WORLD SINCE YOUR CREATION. THE RADIATION THAT POWERS YOU BELONGS TO *ME* NOW.

WHAT ARE YOU--?

GRRAAAHHH!!!

MAJOR FORCE WILL BE DEALT WITH. THE REST OF YOU HAVE *TEN MINUTES* TO EVACUATE THIS CITY. I AM *NOT* MAKING IDLE THREATS.

MR. SPEAKER...VICE PRESIDENT GEKHART... MEMBERS OF CONGRESS... AND MY FELLOW AMERICANS: IN THE NORMAL COURSE OF EVENTS, PRESIDENTS COME TO THIS CHAMBER TO REPORT THE STATE OF THE UNION.

TONIGHT, WE GATHER TOGETHER FOR A DIFFERENT REASON.

"ONE OF OUR CITIES NO LONGER EXISTS."

"IN THE WAKE OF THE UNFATHOMABLE TRAGEDY IN BLÜDHAVEN, OUR FIRST COMMITMENT IS TO MEET THE IMMEDIATE NEEDS OF THOSE WHO FLED THEIR HOMES AND LEFT THEIR POSSESSIONS BEHIND. SADLY, AS A RESULT OF RADIATION POISONING, BLÜDHAVEN WILL NOT--AND CANNOT--BE REBUILT."

"WE HAVE WITNESSED OUR FELLOW CITIZENS LEFT STUNNED AND UPROOTED... GRIEVING FOR THE DEAD AND SEARCHING FOR MEANING IN A TRAGEDY THAT WAS NOT A RANDOM ACT OF NATURE BUT A DELIBERATE ACT BY *METAHUMANS*."

"I SPOKE WITH THE MEMBERS OF CONGRESS THIS MORNING TO DISCUSS THE IMPLEMENTATION OF A GOVERNMENT-SANCTIONED METAHUMAN HOMELAND SECURITY TASKFORCE.

"IN THE ABSENCE OF SUPERMAN, OUR COUNTRY SUFFERED GREATLY. IN FACT, THE EVENTS IN BLÜDHAVEN MARKED A TURNING POINT AND ARE A WAKE-UP CALL NOT ONLY TO AMERICA, BUT THE ENTIRE WORLD.

"TONIGHT I PROPOSE TO YOU THAT WE NEED TO TAKE BACK CONTROL."

KINGDOM COME

Mark Waid and **Alex Ross** deliver a grim tale of youth versus experience, tradition versus change and what defines a hero. KINGDOM COME is a riveting story pitting the old guard — Superman, Batman, Wonder Woman and their peers — against a new uncompromising generation.

WINNER OF FIVE EISNER AND HARVEY AWARDS, INCLUDING BEST LIMITED SERIES AND BEST ARTIST

IDENTITY CRISIS

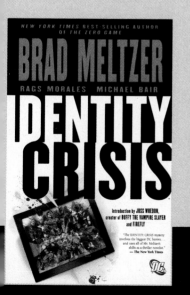

BRAD MELTZER

CRISIS ON INFINITE EARTHS

MARV WOLFMAN

DC: THE NEW FRONTIER VOLUME 1

DARWYN COOKE